EVERYTHING YOU LEFT ME

PAIGE CLASSEY

An imprint of Enslow Publishing

WEST **44** BOOKS™

Please visit our website, www.west44books.com.
For a free color catalog of all our high-quality books,
call toll free 1-800-398-2504.

Cataloging-in-Publication Data

Names: Classey, Paige.
Title: Everything you left me / Paige Classey.
Description: New York : West 44, 2023. |
Identifiers: ISBN 9781978596474 (pbk.) | ISBN
9781978596467 (library bound) | ISBN 9781978596481
(ebook)
Subjects: LCSH: Children's poetry, American. |
Children's poetry, English. | English poetry.
Classification: LCC PS586.3 C537 2023 |
DDC 811'.60809282--dc23

First Edition

Published in 2023 by
Enslow Publishing LLC
2544 Clinton Street
Buffalo, New York 14224

Editor: Caitie McAneney
Designer: Tanya Dellaccio

Photo Credits: Cover vilax/Shutterstock.com; cover font
mikesj11/Shutterstock.com.

Printed in the United States of America

CPSIA compliance information: Batch #CS23W44: For further information contact
Enslow Publishing LLC at 1-800-398-2504.

To my parents,
Tim and Denise Classey,
and my grandparents,
Richard and Dorothy Davidson,
who have always believed I could
be anything I wanted to be.

INTRUDERS

Two uniforms knock
on our front door.

Panic flutters
in the pit
of my stomach.

My mother and I swap a look.
Neither finds an answer.

I CRACK THE DOOR

I've never seen the tall one before.
But the other one is
Dougie Porter.
He looks like a kid playing dress-up.

The tall one says,
"Good morning, ma'am."
His gut spills over
his belt.
A flaky breakfast crumb
clings to his collar.

"Mornin',"
my mother answers.
I hadn't heard her slip
behind me.

"Is this the Morris residence?"
he asks.

My mother
turns to Dougie instead.
"Dougie Porter,
I've known you since you were
in diapers.
You know this is my house."

Dougie scratches his neck.
Mumbles, "Yes, Mrs. Morris.
We just have to do everything by the book,
see."
His eyes sink to the ground.

Was I speeding
on my way home yesterday?
Is this about the graffiti
behind the Dollar-Rama?
Do they think I had something to do
with that?

MIXED UP

Or is Mom
mixed up in drugs
again
and hiding it well?

No More

Officer Crumb Cake
starts again.
"Ma'am, I understand you already know my
partner."
He pauses
to smirk
at Dougie.

"I'm Officer McFarland.
We're looking for an
Edward Leroy Morris.
This house is listed as his last known
address."

Everything stills.
Even the birds stop cawing.

My mother's voice is
quiet.
Cold.
She replies,
"Edward Leroy Morris don't live here
no more."

WHAT KIND OF CRIME

Mom starts to shut the door.

"Do you know his current whereabouts?"

She laughs.
But there is nothing
funny
or warm in it.

"Dougie, what's this about?"
I ask quietly.
He finally looks me in the face.

"Maybeth, we're looking to question him
about his possible involvement
in a crime."

I swallow.
"What kind of crime?"

"I can't tell you that. I'm sorry."

CHILL

Crumb Cake jumps in again.
Thinks he'll have more luck
with me.

"Missy, can you tell me the last time
you saw your daddy?"

I chill my voice
until it's as cool
as my mother's.

"I haven't seen my daddy
since I was eight years old.
That's going on ten years, now.
And it's Maybeth, sir.
Not Missy."

I let the door swing shut in his face.

SURPRISE

Mom raises her eyebrows at me.
Surprised.
I'm a little surprised at myself.

They stand on the front steps
waiting for us to return.
To apologize for our bad manners.
To invite them inside for lemonade
or something.
But eventually they slump back
to the cruiser.

Their car
slips into the flat horizon
as my mind
slips into pieces
of memories.

MY DAD

This is what I remember
of my dad:

Sitting next to him in the big rig.
Splitting a donut.
Him giving me the bigger half.

My mother calling me a *Sass Mouth*.
His big belly laughter in response.
Saying to her, "Diane Fletcher Morris,
where d'you think she got it from?"

Him giving me the pink bicycle
for Christmas.
Used,
but the bell worked.
Streamers hanging from the handlebars.
Him teaching me to ride it
by the end of that afternoon.

Handing him my report card.
All As and *a pleasure to have in class*.
Him cupping my chin in his hand.
Saying, "Baby girl, you're going places in this
world.
You are going to College with a capital C.
Don't you forget it."

And I didn't forget it.
For a while, I thought
College was a place
we would go to together,
in his truck.

I ALSO REMEMBER

The silence
after they argued.
After Dad disappeared for a night or two.

The quiet felt barbed.
Like at any moment
it could cut you.

Weeks of missing him.
Mom shouting into the phone.
Telling him there isn't enough money.
Where is he?
Wasn't he supposed to be back a week ago?

AND HOW
IT ENDED

Waking up to voices
that were trying
and failing
to be quiet
in our ramshackle house.
Cuss words,
words I knew never to say
in front of grown-ups.
Only on the school bus
when the other kids made fun
of my crooked teeth.

I heard the door slam
and the engine roar.
Watched from my window
as his taillights disappeared
into the cold,
flat
night.

PROBABLY

Mom sits down at the kitchen table.
Lights up a cigarette.
I pour myself
another cup of coffee.

"Embezzlement, probably,"
she says.
"He passed a bad check or two
back in the day.
Maybe burglary."
She takes a deep drag.

I shrug a "who cares?"
Then disappear
into my room.

HIDEAWAY PLACES

I set my mug down.
Slip the shoebox out from under my bed.
It may be the most obvious place in the world
to keep a box like this,
but my room is tiny.
Fits a dresser, nightstand, and frilly twin bed.
There just aren't any other
hiding places.

I lift the lid.

MATH

One bike streamer.
One birth certificate.
One report card.
Three photos.
Six postcards
from places like Reno,
Toledo,
Teaneck.
Places I've never been.

Adding each item together
multiplies my love for him.

Even when he's subtracted himself
out of our lives.

THE YEAR AFTER

This is what I remember
of the year after Dad left:

Pretending I didn't want seconds
at dinnertime.

Funny looks
from teachers at school.

Ignoring my bike.

Meeting Lex.

The police picking up my mom
as I watched
from the bus stop.

Mom telling me
they had no proof
of dealing, of anything.

Me calling my mom a liar.
Her spitting the words:
"I did what I had to
to put food in your mouth."

Stuffy ladies from Child Protective Services.
Inspecting my room.
Opening cabinets.
Asking questions
I knew all the right answers to.

The looks on their faces
as they got back in their cars.

The way my heart squeezed
the night I realized
he wasn't coming back

for me.

I SEARCH

Edward Leroy Morris
edward leroy morris missouri
edward morris trucker
edward morris twitter
edward morris facebook

edward leroy morris crimes

I scroll through results:
An elementary school teacher,
a mechanic in Mississippi,
an Ed Morris locked up
for trafficking cocaine
back in 2014.

None seem like him.

But at this point,

would I even know?

LEX

your brother was just here,
I text Lex
(*lexting,* she likes to call it).
Three dots appear.

> *ew why*

here to question me about my dad

> A pause, then,
> *meet at scooters?*

yep

I pull on my rumpled Scooters uniform.
Shove my mom's old phone
into my purse.
Swing out the door.

"Goodbye to you, too!"
my mom barks from the kitchen.

I'm already starting the engine.

SCOOTERS

I pull into the lot.
Figure I have about 15 minutes
before my shift at Scooters:
Jolene's paradise
of frozen food, fryers,
and bathrooms coated in pee.

The smell of greasy onions
wafts through the parking lot.
The people of Jolene file in and out.
A bell chimes each time the door opens.

I feel bone-tired,
and my shift hasn't even
started yet.

VALERIE

Lex rumbles into the lot in Valerie,
her black '95 Camaro.
She rebuilt it herself.
She parks in an empty row facing me.
Lex slips out,
looking just as 90s as her car.
She looks like Fairuza Balk
from *The Craft* today.
All fishnets and dark lipstick.

"Hey, Maypole."
The nickname is a leftover from junior high.
It unfortunately still fits.
I'm five foot nine with no curves in sight.

Lex pulls herself up next to me
on the hood of my car.
The backs of our heels
lightly tap the bumper.

"You don't have to park ten feet away from
me,
you know," I say.
"I won't ding your precious car."

"She has a *name*,
Maybeth," Lex says.
She blows a kiss to Valerie.
Gives her a little wave.

I almost expect Valerie to wave back.

THE WORD

"So *why* was my brother there?"
Lex asks.

"My dad committed some kind of crime,"
I answer.
"Wouldn't say what.
Wanted to know if Mom and I still kept in
touch with him."

She snorts.
Lex is the only one who knows
about the internet searches
and my Dad shoebox.

"Well, crap," she says.
"Like a bank robbery?
Public urination?
Murder?"
Lex spends hours watching shows
about Ted Bundy and all those other creeps.

The word *murder* makes my stomach lurch.

DIGGING

"I'll do some digging,"
Lex says.
Dougie still lives at home,
even though he joined the Jolene PD
last year.

I nod, then add,
"I'm sure it's some kind of fraud
or something."

But I'm not sure at all.

oN MY WAY

The door chimes.
Davey Burt is outside,
hands cupped around his mouth.
"You comin', Maybeth?
We're slammed!"

"Shut up, Davey!
She has five minutes!"
Lex calls across the lot.

I can see the hurt
spreading across Davey's
acne-ridden face.

I give Lex a little shove.

"On my way, Davey."

oNE DAY

Lex slides off my car.
Twirls her keys in one hand.

"Go get 'em, girl.
Save all the details for the
'Growing Up in Nowhere, USA' chapter
of your famous scientist memoir one day."

Thank God for Lex Porter, I think.

MEETING LEX

I met Lex in third grade.
Ms. Callahan's class.
Duncan Wallace
was teasing me for getting another 100
on a spelling quiz.
He told me they must be giving me
the dumbed-down quizzes
since everyone knew
my parents were no-good hicks.

I stared down at my desk,
face on fire,
waiting for it to end.

Until Alexis Porter
leaned in close to Duncan's face.
She snapped, "Oh, shut up, Duncan.
You're just jealous.
Also, your teeth are brown."

ON KINDNESS

Ms. Callahan overheard
and gave Lex a lunch detention
and a lecture
on kindness
and being a proper young lady.

I sat next to her as everyone else played
outside
(including Duncan Wallace).
I couldn't even manage a "thank you."

She passed me her quiz
so I could know for sure
mine was the same
as everyone else's.

BUSY

I spend the hours
whisking away baskets
and ringing up orders
and unjamming the register
and drinking orange sodas
and chatting with the regulars
(retirees, like Bill Beamon
who used to work with my dad),
all to keep my hands busy.
To keep my mind from wandering
into the box
beneath my bed.

THAT NIGHT

I check my phone
over and over.
No lexts.

I play the game I always play
when my mind
won't settle into sleep.

I picture myself
in a cool, white lab.
I'm filling a beaker,
taking notes.

I am alone
in this big, silent building
a million miles from Jolene.

COMMONS

I wait for Lex in the senior commons.
Commons is a fancy name for what is really
just a hallway
the school dedicated to seniors
to try to keep us from vandalizing
teachers' cars
and flushing vapes down the toilets.

I lean against Lex's locker.
Watch the couples stroll past.
Football players
shove each other
back and forth.
Davey chats with a kid
in a cape.
Lindsay Tillerman from AP Bio waves.
I wave back,
let my eyes float elsewhere.
I'm only looking for Lex
this morning.

And there she is,
finally,
at the end of the hall.

NO LUCK

"Hey.
Did you get anything out of Dougie?"

She shakes her head.
"No. I'm sorry.
I harassed him all night.
Wouldn't tell me
a thing."

I sigh.
"Thanks for trying."

HOW IT WILL BE

Maybe this is how it will be.
I'll never know
what they think he did.

It's probably nothing worse
than things Mom's already done
anyway.

PARENTS

"What's it like having parents
that aren't screwups?"
I ask Lex.

Her mother's the churchiest lady I know.
Her dad is (a) around,
and (b) one of the few successful
businessmen
in town.

Probably the most criminal thing
they've ever done
is use the Lord's name
in vain.

And I'm sure they prayed for forgiveness after.

Lex snorts.
"Who says they're not screwups?"

AP BIO

After trying to read T. S. Eliot
in AP Lit
and running half-hearted laps
in the gym,
I sink into AP Bio
like a warm bath.

DOC ANDERSON

Dr. Anderson marks attendance at the front.
There are only eight of us.
When admin tried to shut down the course
due to low enrollment,
Doc Anderson called enough meetings
and stirred up enough parents
to make sure
the school kept it.

She's probably 300 years old
and wears the clothes
of a pioneer woman,
but she can really teach.

And not just how to write a lab report
and the parts of a cell.
The *now* stuff:
disruptions to ecosystems,
advances in genetic engineering.

The world-changing stuff.

AHEAD

She's explaining deviations
in patterns of inheritance
when I glance across the aisle.
I accidentally
lock eyes with
Raquel Tanner.

She gives me a "what are you looking at?"
glare.
Turns back to her notes.
She's second in our class
and has been trying to nudge me out of first
since she moved here
last year.

I always manage to stay
a point
or two
ahead.

ESCAPE HATCH

The valedictorian
of each graduating class
is promised free tuition
upon acceptance
to any state university.

I don't know what Raquel Tanner's story is,
but I can't afford to care.
This is the way out.
The escape hatch.

My only chance.

LUNCH

I slide in across from Lex and Lindsay.
Lex helps herself
to my fries.

"Do you think the grades are gone
for good?" asks Lindsay,
chewing her lip.
She pushes her blue-framed glasses
back up her nose.

"Oh, *heck* yes," says Lex.
"There's no way he's been writing them
down."

Lindsay explains to me,
"Someone hacked Mr. Delphi's gradebook
and we all have As."

As

"Yes, *As*," Lex emphasizes.
"So why do you look so miserable?"

My eyes briefly meet Lindsay's.
Understanding swells between us.
She stays after school
almost every day,
studying
or going for extra help.
She works hard for all her As.
Like I do.

Lex floats through life
on Bs
that she doesn't even have to
try for.
And her parents will pay her way
through any college
she chooses.

AN IDEA

Conversation shifts to prom.
Then to a show I don't watch
because we don't have Netflix.

When Lindsay leaves
to throw away her trash,
Lex leans in and whispers,
"I have an idea."

Her eyes sparkle.
"About how to get the goods
on your dad.
Are you working today
or can you come over
after school?"

Hope surges through me.

TRESPASSING

Lex's house sits
sprawled on the yard
like it knows how good it looks.
My heart always trips
coming up the drive.
I feel like I'm
trespassing.

I park behind Valerie
and follow Lex upstairs.

We pass her oldest brother's room.
He's a grad student at Vanderbilt,
getting his MBA.
Just like the Porters wanted.

Lex keeps moving
down the hall.

To Dougie's room.

DOUGIE'S ROOM

I linger in the doorway.

"He's at the gym, I swear."
Lex sits down at his desk.
Cracks her knuckles.

The trespassing feeling
tingles in my stomach again.
"You're going to log onto his computer?"

"Yep. Thank the joker
who hacked Delphi
for giving me the idea.
This is his work laptop."

"There's no way he told you the password,"
I say.

"Nope.
But I'm going to guess it."
She types and hits enter.
A harsh ding
rings out.

"What makes you so sure?" I ask.

"Because my brother is about as mysterious
as a doorknob."

LEXTING THAT NIGHT

djp12345

?

his password.
douglas james porter 12345
what a moron

you got in??

of course i did

so ...
did u find anything in his history?
lex?
hello??
?????????

SPLIT

Lex is already waiting for me
in Commons the next day.
My stomach sinks
because she doesn't
get to school this early

ever.

"Hey," I say.
I sit down next to her.
The look she gives me
is so full of darkness
that I know my life is about to split in two:

into the Before
and the After,

the Okay Days
and the Very Bad Days,

the Not Knowing

and the Knowing.

DISAPPEARING

"I'm sorry I didn't text you back last night,"
she starts.
"I couldn't
get into the police database,
or whatever.
But I found some articles
in Dougie's history.
Ended up disappearing
down a rabbit hole."
She pinches the bridge of her nose.

TELL ME

"Keep in mind
it could be totally unrelated,
not linked to your dad
at all," she says.

"Just tell me," I say.

"I don't even know
if it's a case he's working on,
or if he's just weirdly interested—"

"Lex."

She spits out,
"Maybeth, there were a ton of searches
for the I-80 Strangler."

THE WHAT

"The—what?"
I ask.

"The I-80 Strangler,"
she says again.

We're not big touchers,
huggers, or anything.
But she reaches over.
Gently squeezes my wrist.
Watches my face.

"It could be nothing.
But a lot of the details …
I don't know.
They think he's a trucker,
since the—
the bodies are all found along the interstate.
He's been active since at least 2010.
That's around when your dad
took off, right?"

GONE

I am listening and not listening.
Everything is the same:
the hallway,
the groups pushing and laughing.
But everything is different, too.
I can't be here.
I need to get out.
Lex is calling my name,
but I'm already gone.

LIBRARY

I am dimly aware
of passing the Dollar-Rama,
Scooters,
churches,
gas stations.
Brown yards
full of dingy
holiday decorations.

I find myself parked
in front of the library.
It's a small brick building
that usually feels warm and comfy,
like an old sweater.
But today the windows
glare at me
like Raquel Tanner.

RESEARCH

I find a quiet corner
and connect my laptop to the Wi-Fi.

I type in "i80 strangler",
which pulls up 12,500,000 results.

My finger hovers over the touchpad.
I breathe in and out
and click on
the top result.

A news article
dated three months ago.

"THE I-80 MURDERS GET A FRESH LOOK"

The article reads:

After years of little movement,
case is re-energized.
September 12, 2022

A road crew was clearing brush
along I-80
in Hastings, Kansas,
in the summer of 2010.
Their flagger
spotted a flash of pink
in the brush.

It was a gruesome discovery:
the remains of a teenage girl,
still wearing jeans
and a pink shirt.

The manner of death was later
determined
to be asphyxiation.

Little to no evidence was found
on the scene.
Authorities suspected
she had been killed elsewhere
and dumped
along the quiet stretch of highway.

THE ARTICLE CONTINUES

She would become known as
Jane Doe Hastings.

Eight more bodies were discovered
along Interstate 80,
a major highway
running from California to New
Jersey.

The victims were female,
ranging from
15 to 32 years old.
The victims had last been seen
at truck stops and convenience
stores.

The cases were finally linked in 2017
when a station out of Indianapolis
broke the story

of a possible serial killer along I-80.

JANE DOE HASTINGS

Hastings PD hired BioTech
to conduct genetic genealogy
to try to uncover the identity
of Jane Doe Hastings.

Their efforts paid off.
After tracing back
from a distant cousin,
investigators were able to confirm
that Jane Doe Hastings
was Brittany Leigh Bates.
A seventeen-year-old
who briefly attended
a nearby high school.

She had been reported missing
by her foster mother.
Her foster family and friends
suspected she had fled back to
her hometown
of Chicopee, Massachusetts.

THE LAST PARAGRAPH

After the identification
was released to the media
this past July,
a tip came in to Hastings PD
that has
reignited the investigation.

The killings stopped
in early 2020,
leading investigators to wonder
if the killer
moved out of the area,
died of COVID-19,
is serving time for an unrelated
crime,

or is biding their time.

THE WORDS I SEE:

remains

dumped

bodies

15 to 32

truck stops

victims

serial killer

HER PICTURE

Brittany is white
with gelled curly hair
and two small studs
in each ear.
Her forced smile reveals
a crooked front tooth
just like mine.
She is holding a
fake flower to her shoulder,
which somehow means
she is on the brink of graduating.

As I stare,
I see glimpses of Lex
in her face.
Lindsay.
Me.

Her eyes tell me
she has no idea
what is about
to happen to her.

Her eyes say,
"Remember me."

OTHER PICTURES

My mind skips to the photos
in my shoebox.
I have studied them
for so long,
it's like they're
spread across my lap.

One is of my mom's parents
who I never met,
grim-faced
at someone's barbeque.

One is of my mom
with her lanky junior prom date.
The year before she met my dad
and ruined her life
by getting pregnant
with me.

THE THIRD PHOTO

The third photo
I rescued from the trash
when my mom purged
his stuff from our house
in a spit-flying rage.

It's the two of us,
sitting in the cab
of his truck.

I am maybe five.

I do the math.
Three years before he left
for good.
A year before
someone did this
horrible thing
to Brittany Leigh Bates.

MY FATHER IS NEXT TO ME

His face is blurred,
like he was turning toward me
when my mother
snapped the photo.
His floppy hair is tucked
under a baseball hat.
A bristly beard covers
his chin.

He smiles down
at the top of my head.

Is this the man who
killed them?

Is this truck where
he killed them?

Am I the daughter
of the man
who killed them all?

PANIC

My chest tightens.
The edges of my vision
crackle.

A small voice
in the back of my head
that sounds like Doc Anderson
says, "Hyperventilation."

I cling to the word.
Define it:
abnormal breathing.
Increased removal of carbon dioxide
from the blood.

The most common cause:
anxiety.

SLOW

I can control this, I think.
Slow down your breathing.

Slow.
Down.
Your.
Breathing.

SCIENCE

I force my mind to think of
Doc Anderson's lab.
My quiet bedroom.

Breathe.

My pulse races
but my vision is clearing.
I feel a sense of calm
start to lap at my fingers.

A knowledge of science
working to help me
in my everyday life.

And that's when I land on it:
science will help me
prove them wrong
about my father, too.

I DON'T BOTHER

I don't bother
going back to school.

I don't bother
picking up my phone.
It's buzzing away
with texts and calls
from Lex and Lindsay.

I don't bother
waking my mother,
who's sleeping on the couch
before her night shift
at the old people's home.

I don't bother
eating
drinking
changing
calling out of work.

I plug my laptop back in
and get started.

LAB REPORT

TITLE:
Proving Them Wrong

ABSTRACT:
I'll write this last.
I can't summarize findings
I don't have yet.

INTRODUCTION:
The problem being studied
is that the police
are blaming my dad
for things
he couldn't have done.
My hypothesis?
Someone else spent ten years
destroying lives
and they deserve to pay for it.

METHODS AND MATERIALS:
One laptop.
Internet access.
Interviews.
A map of the United States

Step 1: Write questions.
Step 2: Find answers.
Step 3: No idea.

RESULTS:
TBD

DISCUSSION:
TBD

CONCLUSION:
TBD

QUESTIONS

When was the killer active?
  2010–2020, nine murders total
  (I was six when it started—
  he was still living with us.)

Any patterns in victims' identities?
  No.
  Young women.
  Some involved in sex work.
  Some running errands.
  Some running away.
  Based on the photos,
  they were different races,
  different builds.

Any forensic evidence available in the case?
  Little to none (they claim).
  No weapons,
  fibers,
  hairs,
  bite marks,
  unusual vegetation,
  fingerprints,
  shoe prints,
  tire tracks,
  nothing.

How did they identify my dad as a suspect?
  Unclear.

What were his usual routes?
  Ask Bill Beamon.

MESSAGES

When I wake up the next morning,
my laptop is dead in my bed.
Mom isn't back yet.

I plug in my charger
and start a pot of coffee.

I have a zillion missed calls
and lexts.

are you ok??
seriously call me
im at your house where r u
ANSWER ME IF YOU'RE ALIVE
im at scooters
you're missing your shift
MAYBETH

I have a text
from Lindsay.

hey aren't you in school today?
bio quiz starting now

NO LONGER MATTER

I think fleetingly
of the quiz I missed.
How ready I was to write about
meiosis and gene expression and a million
other things
that no longer matter
at all.

SCOOTERS, PART TWO

Bill's Chevrolet is parked out front.
He's in his usual booth,
sipping coffee.
He'll be back again around 4:30
for a chicken sandwich.
Good old, reliable Bill Beamon.

BILL

I slide in opposite him.
I don't think
my manager
can see me.
Bill sputters on
a mouthful of coffee.
Presses a napkin to his mouth.

"Maybeth!
Good Lord, you near
startled me right out of my skin."
His smiling eyes
squint suspiciously.
"What are you doing working
during the school day?"

He's leaning into the aisle
to scold the manager
for bringing me in,
but I reach for his wrist.

"Mr. Beamon, I'm not working right now.
I was hoping you'd be able to answer
a couple of questions for me."
I let go.

"About my dad."

PITY

Pity blooms in his eyes.
He rubs a hand
over his cheek and jaw.

"Oh, well now.
I haven't spoken to your daddy
in years,
but I'll try to answer
any question you might have."

He folds his hands in his lap.
The look on his face is so sincere,
I could kiss him.

"Thank you,
Mr. Beamon. Really."

"Bill. Please," he says.

"Thank you, Bill," I say.

TRUCKING

I think back to the questions
I brainstormed.

"Remind me of the name
of the company
you and my dad worked for?"

He touches a finger
to the brim of his hat.
WYLAND FREIGHT INC.
is printed across the front.

"Right. Wyland."
I think about the best way
to get him talking.
"Did you—like working there?"

"Like it? I loved it!" he exclaims.
"Miles and miles of freedom.
They took good care of their workers then,
too.
Good money and benefits.
Not like how it is nowadays,
with all the sensors and tracking.
Louanne and I were able to buy our first
home.
That's a really wonderful thing
about this country—"

BACK ON TRACK

"Did you travel the whole country?
Or just the Midwest?"

"Oh, I've been near 'bout everywhere.
All the major routes.
Even did a stint up and down 95
for a while,
Maine to Florida."

"Was one of your routes
I-80?"

He nods.
"Yes, ma'am. I ran I-80
all the time."

FAINT HOPE

"Do you remember
if my dad ran I-80?"

"I'm sure he did," he says.

My heart trembles.

He adds,
"But only because every trucker
in the Midwest has run I-80
at some point or another."

"It's a common route?" I ask.

"Oh, the most common you get out here."

I feel a faint hope
flicker in my chest.
It's a major highway.
Tons of truckers use it
every day, every year.

ONE MORE THING

Bill leans
across the table.
"I don't know if it's my place
to say this,
seeing as how I didn't know your dad
too well.
We were always out on the road,
only talked through the CB.
But he had a picture of you
hanging from his rearview mirror.
I think your daddy really
loved you."

I choke back the sob
that's about to tear out of my throat.

"Thanks for saying that, Bill.
I think he did, too."

FOUND OUT

I spend the afternoon at the library,
zooming in and out
on a map of the United States.
I google Wyland
and my dad's name.
Still no news stories
tying him to all of this.

When I pull up to the house,
Mom's sitting on the steps,
smoking and jiggling her foot.

"Maybeth Diane Morris,
where have you been?"

I try to hurry past her up the steps.
She grips my shoulder.
Turns me to face her.

"Answer me!"

INCONVENIENCE

"I was out," I say.

"Out?
What kind of an answer
is that?"
She follows me
into my room.

"You scared me half to death.
The school called.
I had no idea what they were talking about.
I picked up overtime
and had to leave!
You know I can't leave work."

"Sorry to inconvenience you, Mom,"
I say.
I focus on a spot
just beyond her ear.

Her face stills
with a new layer of rage.

CARE

"Where have you been?" she asks.

"Why do you care?" I throw back at her.

My mom opens her mouth,
but I'm already yelling.

"Really, why do you care?
You're never home.
When you are, you're asleep.
You never gave a crap about school,
so why should I?"

Confusion settles
into her eyes.
"Because you love school.
You always have."

NOT ANYMORE

"Well, I don't anymore.
It's a waste of time.
I won't graduate.
I won't go to college.
I'll stay here forever
in this garbage heap of a town
and be just like you.
Just like you always wanted."

WHAT I WANT

"That is not
what I want."
Mom's voice is a whisper.

"Really?" I say.
"Well, you could have fooled me.
You never ask what I'm learning.
You never come to school for anything.
I only ever tried because Dad thought—
and now—"

"And now what?
What's goin' on, Maybeth?"
Mom perches on the edge of my dresser.

I open my mouth
but my thoughts are
mixing and jumbling.

I lie down on my bed,
yell, "Get out.
Just get out!"

A pause, but then
the door clicks softly shut
behind her.

PEACE OFFERING

Hot tears run
down my face
until I nod off.
When I wake again,
gray light peeps in
from under my blinds.

I pad out to the kitchen.
Mom's already left,
but there's a package of Pop-Tarts on the
table
and a note that says,
"Get your butt to school today.
I love you.
—Your mom"

I smile.
Slip the Pop-Tarts
into my backpack.

It's the Friday before
the holidays.
I'll go in today
and figure this out
over break.

LEX TRACKS ME DOWN IN PE

She sits next to me
as we stretch.

"Are you lost, Ms. Porter?
You don't have my class
today."
Coach Bart frowns into his jowls.

"Oh, I know, Coach.
Just needed to get a good stretch in
before lunch."
His frown deepens.

"Five minutes, young lady,
then off you go."

"Yes, sir!" Lex salutes him,
then flips her middle finger
to his retreating back.

"Where have you been?
Did your mom call you out?
Did you forget how to use a phone?"

HE COULDN'T HAVE

"I'm sorry.
I meant to respond.
I needed a few days
to get my thoughts together."

Coach Bart stares at us.
We reach out to touch our toes.

"Okay, and …
what are your thoughts?"

I lower my voice.
"That he couldn't have done
any of this.
He just isn't capable.
There were no signs.
No abuse."

She doesn't look convinced.

HE COULDN'T HAVE, PART TWO

"He was still living with us
when the murders started.
We would have known.
Or at least my mom would have
and turned him in.
You can't just hide
something like that.
Torn clothes,
restraints—"
I wince.

"He was totally normal.
He'd let me play in the truck
all the time.
If he was murdering people in there,
would he really have let me do that?"

She picks at the hem
of her shirt.

"If they had anything real on him,
it would be all over the news," I say.

"I guess that's true.
If they were sure,
there'd be a manhunt on by now."
Lex stands up.
"I better get out of here
before Coach Fart circles back.
Catch you at lunch."

MANHUNT

The word *manhunt*
stays with me
the rest of the day.

AFTER CLASS
WITH DOC

"I noticed you were out yesterday.
And the day before that."

"Yes, ma'am." I hang my head.

"You're never absent.
And the absences were marked
unexcused."

It's a statement
but also a question,
one I don't know how to answer.
I don't want to lie
and pretend I was sick,
but I also can't tell her
about my dad.

My eyes suddenly
burn with tears.

ERROR

"Clearly an error
in the main office,"
she says,
softly.
"Why don't we schedule a time
for you to make up
your quiz
after break?
You can get the notes
from a classmate.
Ms. Tillerman, perhaps."

I thank her
and rush out the door.

DAVEY

Davey catches me on my way
down the science wing.
"Hey, where were you
the other night?
You left us high and dry
at the Scoot, Maybeth!"

"Just leave me alone,
Davey."

I shove past him
before I can see
the look on his face.

ON CHRISTMAS EVE EVE

We meet in Lex's basement.
Lindsay lets me borrow her notes
while she starts college applications.
Lex surfs the web
for car parts.
On TV, Will Ferrell
decorates a department store.

"Aren't you going to apply
somewhere?" Lindsay asks.

Lex shrugs.
"My cousin Greg said I could come
work in his shop next year."

My eyes meet Lindsay's.

"What do your parents think
about that?" I ask.
I can hear Mrs. Porter a floor above us,
baking cookies in her sparkling kitchen.

"I don't care
what my parents think
about that,"
says Lex,
and we leave it alone.

THE WAY HOME

Lindsay is applying to college.
Lex has made plans, too.
And what have I been doing?

Spiraling about my dad
who hasn't cared
about me
for the last decade.

I need
to get back
on track.

PROMPTS

I fill in my name,
birth date,
address,
high school.
So far, so good.

Until the essay prompts.

ALL WRONG

Recount a time when you faced
an obstacle
and how you dealt with the situation.

Well, I found out the police think
my dad is a serial killer.
I reacted by cutting school
and screaming at my mom.

Reflect on a time when you
questioned a belief.

I believed my dad was good,
that I was smart,
that I could make it,
but maybe I had it
all wrong.

I shove my computer
aside.
Turn the TV
back on.

CHRISTMAS

Mom gives me
a new bathrobe,
shower caddy,
and laundry bag.

"For dorm living,"
she clarifies,
eyes on the floor
as she sips her coffee.

The real gift
is knowing she does want me
to go away to school
after all.

She loves the weighted blanket
I've wrapped for her—
a little bit of comfort
for the most overworked person
I know.

We stay in our pajamas all day.
We order Chinese
and fall asleep watching movies
on the couch.

THE KNOCK

I'm in my room,
starting an essay
on how Doc Anderson
has played a pivotal role
in my life,
when the knock comes.

I already know
who it is.

INTRUDERS, PART TWO

I peek into the living room.
Watch as my mom
cracks the door.

It's Officer Crumb Cake again.
"Good afternoon, Ms. Morris.
We were hoping to ask you
a few more questions about Mr. Morris,
if you don't mind."

"I do mind," Mom says.
"I'm heading out the door
to work."
This is a lie.
Mom doesn't go in
for another three hours.

"It'll just take a few moments, ma'am."

There's a long beat
before she gives in
and holds the door open.

FEDS

No Dougie this time.
Instead, Crumb Cake is followed in
by two men in polo shirts
and expensive sunglasses.

Federal agents.
In our house.

HER MOMENT

As much as I want
to burrow back into my room,
I can't let my mother
face this alone.

Crumb Cake ignores me.
The feds track me as I cross the room
and sit down next to my mom.

"This is my daughter, Maybeth."

The taller agent
with the shaved head
opens his mouth.
My mother cuts him off.

"She can hear whatever it is you have
to say to me."

Her voice is tough,
but her hand trembles
as she lights her cigarette.

This is her moment
between the Before
and the After.

IN THAT MOMENT

I want to reach back through the years
to before my mom had me at nineteen,
to before she met him,
to when she was just a kid
with long braids
racing her friends through
the tall, tall grass.
I want to tell her
to keep running
and don't look back.

Instead, I reach for her hand.

SAMPLE

"I'm Special Agent Miller.
This is Special Agent Robideau."

The shorter one with blue-gray eyes
flashes his badge.
Mom nods for them to take a seat
at the table with us.
She grips my hand tighter.
There aren't enough chairs for Crumb Cake.
He leans against the wall,
looking put out.

"Mrs. Morris," Miller starts.

"Diane, please."

"Diane, we're here to see
if you would allow us to take a DNA sample
from your daughter."

My breath catches.

"As Maybeth is still a minor,
we would need your written consent.
And hers as well."

SPECIMEN

I think suddenly of the animals
we've studied in bio,
the tapeworms and fetal pigs,
their bodies splayed open
as we probed inside
with our knives and tweezers.

NEVER

"For what possible reason
could you need my daughter's DNA?"
Mom's voice is soft and timid.
It is only then
that I realize the size
of my mother's fear.
She is never soft.
Never timid.

Robideau jumps in.
"Your ex-husband
is under investigation
for a series of murders
committed in six states."

We all watch my mom
absorb this information.
A twitch pulses beneath
her left eye.
I want her to scream at them
that they've got the wrong guy.

NINE

Instead, she asks,
"How many murders?"
At least the softness
is gone from her voice.

"Nine."

MATCH

"You have the killer's DNA?"

Robideau and Miller trade
a look.
"We are currently retesting evidence
from the crime scenes."

"So the answer is no," she says.

"No.
But we are hopeful.
The advances in testing—"

"And if you find any,
you hope to match it
to my daughter's."

PARASITE

Suddenly, I can feel every blood cell
surging through my body,
every twisting DNA strand.
I can feel my father's genes
lurking underneath my skin
like a parasite.
I let go
of my mom's hand
and dig my nails
into my palms
to stop myself
from shredding the skin
off my arms.

CERTAIN

She coughs.
"For a couple of people
without DNA,
you sound pretty certain
it was him."

The silence that follows
speaks volumes.

MAY AS WELL

Crumb Cake folds his arms
across his chest.
"You may as well tell them.
It's going to be all over the news
soon enough."

I look gratefully at Crumb Cake,
Officer McFarland.
However bad it is,
we need to know.
Will they tell us
about the tip
mentioned in the article?

WITNESS

Miller's voice is kinder
when he says,
"After we were able to identify
one of the victims—"
(Brittany Leigh Bates's senior photo
flashes before me)
"—a witness called in a tip.
A former acquaintance
of the victim.
She had seen the victim willingly
get into a truck
at a truck stop.

She jotted it down in a diary
because the whole thing seemed fishy.
Left town soon after.
Forgot all about it
until the identification
was released to the media
last summer."

Robideau leans forward.

"She found the diary.
She'd written 'Wyland.'
And the license plate."

THAT'S WHEN
I KNOW

My mom hisses,
"But they shared trucks all the time!
He didn't drive just one truck."

Miller's eyes darken.
"We followed up with Wyland.
They checked their records,
their log books.
It was him that day.
And he left the company
just before they
started using GPS tracking."

Robideau quietly adds,
"We don't think
the timing
was a coincidence."

Mom deflates in her chair.

And that's when I know
for sure.

CONCLUSION

I was wrong.
He did this.
He did all of this.

I am the daughter
of a serial killer.

And science will prove it.

EVIDENCE

My mom tells me
we don't have to do it.
But I sign the paperwork.
She signs it, too.

They swab the inside
of my mouth.
I think about the test tube
the swab will end up in.
It will be stored
in a lab,
ready to be matched
if the time comes.

This whole time
I thought
I would be the scientist,
not the guinea pig.

I almost laugh
at how stupid I've been.

BEFORE THEY LEAVE

They tell us there will be
a press conference tomorrow.
They need the public's help
in locating my father
for questioning.

Everyone will know.

Robideau asks,
"Ma'am, do you happen to have
anything that belonged
to Mr. Morris?
Any personal effects
you may have held onto?"

I think of the box
underneath my bed.
Can practically hear it
calling my name.

My mother sneers,
"No. I did not keep
any of his *personal effects*.
Good riddance."

I feel Miller's eyes on me
for a moment,
but they say goodbye.
They take my DNA with them.

WE STAND IN
THE KITCHEN

"You knew," she says.
It's not a question.

"Lex hacked into Dougie's computer."

My mom licks her lips.
I tense,
ready to tell her
I was protecting her.
I didn't want her to know
until she had to.

INSTEAD

Instead, she opens her arms.
We hold each other
in the sunlight
falling into our kitchen.

We cry
and she rocks us gently
back and forth.

"I'm so sorry,"
she says,
again and again.
"I'm so sorry."

THE WATER TOWER

I climb the ladder
up to the water tower
and wait for Lex.
It's our New Year's Eve tradition.
Lex says it reminds us
there's a whole world out there.

She parks Valerie on the grass
and a pop of fuchsia
emerges from the car.

"New year,
new hair,
new me!" she says,
striking a pose.

"I love it," I call.

She climbs up onto the platform
and sits.

The flat prairie
stretches on and on.
From up here,
our town looks almost beautiful.

OVER

"Our last New Year
of high school," Lex says.

"You almost sounded sad
for a minute there."

"Nah," she says,
raking her fingers
through her new hair.
"Just ready
for it to be over, already."

"Same."

I take a deep breath
and tell her
about our visit
from the FBI.

POSTCARDS

After I finish,
Lex is quiet.

"At least my mom knows now.
And she and I are on good terms,
for once."

Lex is still quiet.

"What?" I ask.

"Why didn't you give them
the postcards?" she asks.

It's a valid question,
but I feel my hackles rise.

LOCATIONS

"DNA from a postcard
isn't the same as DNA on a—
a victim."
I stumble over the word.
"Plus, they have mine."

"But what about
the locations?"

I stammer,
"What do you mean,
'locations'?"

She says,
"Where they were sent from.
What if they can tie him
to any of the towns
where the bodies were found?"

BREAKING

I have been so wrapped up in DNA,
I somehow missed this.
Reno.
Toledo.
Where else?
How many times have I read those
postcards?

The thought of Robideau's gloved fingers
sealing them into a plastic bag
cracks something inside me.

MINE

"They're mine.
He sent them to *me*.
They're all I have left
of him.
I can't just—
give them away."

I hear how weak and childish
it sounds.

But I don't care.

FAMILIES

"But what if they can help
solve this?
What about the
families?"

I spit out,
"What about *my* family?
What about what happens
to me and my mom
if it ends up being him?"

She looks as if
I've hit her in the face.

"Maybeth, the truth is the truth.
You have to think about
the greater good."

RIPPLES

"You don't know what you're talking about,
Lex."

"No?"

"No," I say. "Your family is perfect.
Your parents are together.
They love you.
They're rich.
You could go to school anywhere you want.
Do anything you want.
And you don't even appreciate it."

I see the hurt
ripple across
her face,
even in the dark.

RESPONSIBILITY

But then her eyes narrow.
"You don't know anything
about my family.
And it doesn't change the fact
that your dad
needs to be held
responsible."

I say some more words
I know I'll regret.
I scramble down the water tower.
She doesn't try to stop me.

THE SAME ME

I drive
and drive
and drive.

Finally,
I pull over.
Beat the steering wheel.
Scream.

The clock
flips to midnight.

It's a new year
but I'm still
the same me.

THE FIRST POSTCARD

He sent it
just a few weeks after
he left.
It's dated November 3, 2012.

"Miss ya, baby girl!
Keep doing good in school
and help your mama.
Love,
YOUR DAD"

My eyes
find the return address.

All it says
is Ed Morris,
Toledo, Ohio.

I Google
"I80 strangler, ohio, 2012"
and hold my breath.

1 HOUR, 51 MINUTES

Rhonda Royce,
murdered on November 2, 2012
in Cleveland.

My fingers shaking,
I search how far it is
from Cleveland to Toledo.

1 hour, 51 minutes.

I close the screen.

PRESS CONFERENCE

Mom has it on low,
but I can still hear
most of it
from my room.

His name.
Wanted for questioning.
He may have information
they seek.
Blah
blah
blah.

I spend New Year's Day
in bed,
staring
at
the
ceiling.

BACK TO SCHOOL

I'm at school early
to make up my quiz.
I feel eyes on me
the second I park.
I hear whispers.

Lex will show up soon,
so Commons is not
an option.

The bile rising
in my throat
pushes me
into the bathroom.
I cram my stuff into the last stall
and lock the flimsy door behind me.
I sit on the toilet seat
and fight the urge
to dry heave.

COMPLAINTS

The bathroom door swings open
and two pairs of sneakers
echo off the tile.

"You should complain
to Guidance."

I don't know this voice,
but the one that responds
is Raquel's.

"I really should.
Being the daughter of a
serial murderer
should, like, automatically disqualify you
from college.
Let alone from being
valedictorian."

SHE CUTS DEEPER

Raquel's words slice
through the room.

"I just want to say to her,
give up already.
You're not going to be anything
anyway.
She'll end up pregnant next year
like her mom.
Or too busy *killing* people like her dad.
And I'll just be like: see?"

My throat
starts to close.

"The scholarship
will be wasted on her.
And I'll be paying giant loans
for the next decade."

The last few words
trail away
as they head back out
into the hall.

I CAN'T BREATHE

I gasp for breath
but there's not enough air.
I can't breathe
in this town,
in this school,
in this no-good body
of mine.

STUDIES

I pull myself together
and make it to Doc Anderson's room
five minutes late.

The quiz is all free-response questions
based on figures
for the AP exam.
I have to read the question
about mitochondrial DNA
in bear populations
three times
before I can muffle the sound of
Raquel's words
ringing through my head.

I sketch out
the phylogenetic tree
and support my answer
with evidence.
I check it over
before I turn it in.

Doc studies me carefully
over the rims of her glasses.

STRENGTH

"Is everything alright,
Maybeth?"

She's probably seen
the press conference.

I summon
the strength
to ask the question
that's been swimming through
my brain, my veins,
since the FBI
showed up.

INHERITANCE

"I'm wondering if you could tell me
if evil is genetic.
I mean, like criminal behavior.
Or the … the need
to hurt others?
Can that be …
inherited?"

I feel like whatever she says next
is going to determine
the rest
of my life.

ANSWERS

She steeples her fingers together.
"Yes and no.

There's no easy answer
to your question.
There have been some studies,
in males,
suggesting the level of a certain enzyme
may be linked
to a tendency toward violence.
But only when mixed
with certain environmental factors.
Like abuse, neglect.

There are ongoing studies
about brain injuries.
How they might lead someone
toward … what you call evil."

SHOCK

Her voice is quiet
when she adds,
"But there are many people
who get brain injuries,
who are raised in awful homes,
who don't go on
to hurt others."

And then she really
shocks me.

"Did your mother ever tell you
I had her in class?"

FIRST LAUGH

"Wow. No.
My mom and I
don't talk about school
much," I say.

"They had me teaching
two sections of
freshman Earth Science
back then.
Can you imagine?"

She rolls her eyes,
like, *Can you even believe
they made me suffer
that indignity?*

I laugh
for the first time
in weeks.

YOUR MOTHER

"Your mother was bright, funny.
Used to pass notes
in my class
when she thought
I wasn't looking.
She did her homework,
though.
Got a B+ in the class."

I try to imagine my mom
sitting in this lab
or one like it,
getting a B+
in Earth Science.

I can't.

HOPSCOTCH

"I was disappointed
when she decided
not to apply to college.
But from what I hear,
she's been working at Twin Pines
for quite a while,
correct?"

I nod.
She nods back,
thoughtfully.

"I learned she had you
just a year after graduating.
I saw the two of you together
twice,
when you were very little.
Once from across the pharmacy.
You were a baby,
sick with something or other.
She was singing to you,
rubbing your back
while you wailed away
in her ear."

She leans forward
in her chair.
"And then I saw you
at the Food Mart, a few years later.
She was hopscotching
with you down
the aisle."

ONES LIKE THESE

When she says this,
memories jar loose.
My mom and I used to do that
everywhere:
in parking lots,
waiting rooms,
our driveway.

I wonder
why I recall the bad memories
of my mother
so clearly, so easily.
Instead of ones like these.

GOOD PERSON

"You are a good person, Maybeth.
You care about others.
There is nothing evil
about you."

I flash to Lex's face
just before I climbed down
the water tower.
To Davey's
when I blew him off
in the hallway.
To my mom's
when I screamed at her.

Shame pricks
the back of my eyes.

SO MUCH
TO OFFER

"But if you are going to walk away
from this conversation
believing your parents determine
who you are,
then you can't ignore
the role your friends and mother
have played.
You can't ignore
the hopscotch
down the aisle."

I swallow down
the lump growing
in my throat.

"I'd *prefer* you to walk away
knowing that
what's going on with your father
should not make you question yourself
for one minute.
You are smart
and strong
and have so much
to offer this world."

EVEN IF

Even if my brain is fine,
even if my mom loves me,
even if I don't hurt anyone
for the rest of my life …

I will still get to live that life
when his victims can't.

I will breathe air
and laugh
and grow up
while his victims won't.

Where is the fairness
in that?

How will the victims' families feel
when they learn
he has a daughter?

Who will be able to
stand me
when I can't even
stand myself?

THE LONGEST SCHOOL DAY

I pass Lex just once
that day.
She seems to be the only person
in the whole school
who isn't glaring
or laughing at me.
Lex stares through me
like I'm nothing.

Lindsay asks
if I want to meet up later
to look at each other's
college essays.
I'm too embarrassed
to tell her
I still haven't written mine.
I have work
the next few nights,
so we plan to meet
Saturday
at the library.

FINAL BELL

The final bell rings
and I run to my locker.
As soon as it opens,
papers spill out
onto the floor.

Printouts of
Brittany Leigh Bates
and Rhonda Royce
and five or six
other women
smile up at me
from the floor.

FAR FROM THE TREE

One paper
is my junior year picture
sporting devil horns.
A caption
underneath says:
"THE APPLE
DOESN'T FALL FAR
FROM THE TREE."

I look around.
Everyone pretends
not to be watching me.

I slam my locker shut
and wait until I'm in my car
before I start sobbing.

BLUR

Work is a blur.
No one mentions
my missed shift.

Davey leaves an orange soda
next to my register
and smiles at me.

I whisper "thank you"
and bustle into the back
for more ketchup.

LINDSAY AT THE LIBRARY

I look up
after finishing
Lindsay's essay,
not sure where to begin.

"Well?" she asks.

"Well,
you're definitely a writer," I say.
"I was totally swept away."

She grins.
Her eyes gleam
behind her glasses.

Her essay
on why she plans to become a journalist
is completely convincing.
I had no idea
she could write
like this.

I had no idea
about a lot of Lindsay's life.

WHAT WE SHARE

"These parts about
how hard it's been for you,
growing up here."
I swallow.
"I'm sorry I never realized.
Or thought to ask."

She shrugs.
"My brother and I
are the only multiracial kids
that I know of
in this entire town.
Of course it's been hard."

She looks at me very carefully.
"I know Lex is your best friend.
But you're not the only one
dying to get out of here.
Let's help each other
as much as we can."

SHE'S RIGHT

It's always been me and Lex,
Lex and me.
Lindsay has been
an afterthought.
And here she is,
spending her Saturday
at the library,
avoiding the subject of my dad,
sharing this glimpse
of herself
with me.

"But really," she says.
"What can I improve?
Get picky, now.
I need those acceptance emails
rolling in."

I smile.
Point out a word she repeated.
A place that could use
a one-sentence paragraph,
like we practiced in Lit.

It's all I can come up with.

MY ESSAY

is nonexistent.

TRUST

"Nothing?" Lindsay asks.

"Nothing."

I rest my forehead
in my hand.

"I've tried a few times
to write about Doc
being my role model.
But I just can't concentrate—"

I hesitate,
but choose to trust,
like she's trusted me.
"—on anything other
than this stuff with my dad."

"Then write about that," she says.

The look on my face
makes her laugh.

"Really.
Write about
what you care about."

LIGHTER

"Who would accept me?
The daughter of a probable serial killer?"

Saying it out loud
makes me feel
sick,
but also a little
lighter.

THREE REASONS

"First of all,
that's not all you are.
Second,
it makes you stand out."

She points her pen at me.
"And third,
if you can't stop worrying about it,
it might help
to write about it."

I TAKE
HER ADVICE

That afternoon
while Mom snoozes
on the couch,
I close the door to my room
and open a new document.

I watch the cursor blink.
Then I type:
"Halfway through my senior year,
I discovered my father
was being investigated for murder."

CHOSEN

I don't stop to worry over spelling
or word choice.
I just write.

And I discover something
I didn't know.

"I've always wanted
a career in science.
And now I want
to help victims
and their families.
I want to help stop
people like my father.

Instead of choosing forensics,
it feels like forensics
has chosen me."

BLOCKED

Lindsay was right.
I have a first draft,
one that feels like me.
I'm getting up
to grab a snack
when my phone buzzes.

The number is blocked.

My first thought
is that it's some kind of telemarketer.
My second thought
is that maybe it's Lex,
calling from someone else's phone.
She's done it before.

"Hello?"

VAGUELY FAMILIAR

"Maybeth?"

It's a man's voice
that feels vaguely familiar,
like it belongs to
an old teacher
or a regular
from Scooters.

"Yes?"

There's a long pause.
I'm ready to hit end,
but then the caller says,

"Maybeth, it's your dad."

NUMB

I wait for the caller
to burst out laughing.
To realize that it's just
some jerk from school
playing a prank.
But there's no sound.

Only my own
too-loud breathing.

"How did you get this number?"

"I saw online your mom has a new number.
I thought maybe
she gave you
her old one."

My whole body
goes numb.

SO LONG

"It's so good
to hear your voice,
baby girl.
You sound so grown up!
I've missed you so much."

Words I've waited
so long
to hear.

LOUD

I try to say
something,
anything.

The silence
grows loud
between us.

MISTAKES

"Honey, what they're saying
on the news …
it's not true.
I need you to know that.
It's all a mistake.
But I'm in trouble.
I need your help.
Are you alone right now?"

BELONGING(S)

I must make some kind of sound,
because he goes on.

"Did your mother keep
any of my stuff?
My belongings?
I left a passport
at our house."

Our house.
He says it
like he left his lunch box
on the counter
this morning.
Anger
brings me back
to myself.

"No, Dad,"
I snap into the phone.
"No, we didn't keep
any of your *belongings*.
We threw everything out."

I swear I can hear
the shoebox
rattling under
my bed.

CHOKING

He hears the blade
in my voice.
His voice
goes soft
like a hug.

"I understand.
I know I hurt you both
so, so bad.
I can't ever
begin to make it up to you."
There's a gulp,
like he's choking back
tears.

"I'm sorry I bothered you.
I'll leave you alone,
keep you out of this
awful mess …"

WAIT

My heart lurches.

"Wait," I say.
"Don't go."

TO BE HONEST

"I'll check for the passport.
What else do you need?"

He asks me to look
for his social security card.
Then mentions
he could use a few more blankets.
A flashlight.
Any cash
I could spare.

"Are you heading north
or south?"
Canada or Mexico.

"Well, to be honest,
I'm not quite sure yet.
Taking this one step at a time.
I'm hoping it all
gets straightened out
before I have to go anywhere!"
A rumbling laugh.

I can feel the lie
lurking under
his words.

He knows
and won't say.

THE SPOT

"Where should I meet you?"

I imagine what it would be like
to watch him pull up next to me.
Would he be shocked to see me
all grown up?
Would he recognize himself
in my face?

"Is it still pretty empty
out by Wyland?
I could meet you near
that stretch of woods
just past it.
You know the spot?"

I nod.
Force myself to say, "Yes."

PROMISES

"Great.
And Maybeth—
I hate to ask you this,
but please keep it
to yourself.
It's important that I get on out
as fast as I can."

"I won't tell anyone."

I wonder
if he's ever kept a promise
in his whole life.

"When?"

"Tonight.
Around eight?"

Three hours.
He could be here
in just three hours.

MY BRAIN

My brain catalogs
the evidence
against him:

the witness
the postcards
leaving Wyland
when they started
tracking trucks
his familiarity
with I-80
his lack of online presence
his lack of my-life presence
fleeing the country

VERSUS MY HEART

But my heart cries:

donuts
the bike
college with a capital C
baby girl!

He called you.
He loves you.
He needs your help.

WHAT HAPPENS

What happens to my dad
if I turn him in?
Or if I don't?

What happens to me
if I turn him in?

Or if I don't?

WHAT I NEED

I fill an old backpack
with what I need
and slip silently
out the front door.

I DRIVE

I drive past
Scooters,
the library,
the turnoff
for Lex's house.

I drive past Wyland,
all shadows
in the setting sun.

I drive.

SAFE

As I glance
in my rearview mirror,
I wonder about my school picture
that used to hang
from his truck's rearview mirror,
the one Bill remembered.

Did it say to the women:
"See? I'm a dad.
I'm safe.
You're safe with me."

ON HIS WAY

When I ask for Dougie,
the officer eyes me
and my backpack carefully,
but she leads me inside.

It could almost be
a regular office
except for the room
with the cell.

Dougie shoots up from his seat.

"Maybeth!
Is everything okay?"

I drop the backpack
in the center of his desk.

"He's on his way
to Jolene.
We don't have much time."

DETAILS

He motions for me
to sit.

I clear my throat.
I'm tired of hiding
in bathroom stalls
and crying in my car.

"He called me.
Asked me to meet him
with his passport
and some other supplies.
Out by Wyland
at eight o'clock."

BACKPACK

I pull out the six postcards.

The ones that will connect my dad to:

Rhonda Royce in Cleveland,
2012.

Emily Howard and Crystal King
outside Teaneck,
2014.

I throw my cell phone
on the pile, too.

TIME

"You'll maybe get his DNA
from under the stamps.
Two of the postcards
place him near ...
where they found
some of the bodies."

Dougie's eyes
lift to mine.

I stare right back.
"You don't have much time."

LIGHT

I show Dougie the spot
on a map.
He's calling Miller
as I leave.
McFarland rushes past in the lobby
and tips me a grateful nod.

Out in the parking lot,
I gulp the icy air.

I feel
so light
without the backpack
weighing me
down.

PARKING LOT

I'm leaning against Valerie
when Lex walks out
of kickboxing class.

I pick myself off
her driver's side door.

"I gave the postcards to your brother."

Silence stretches between us.
I try again.

"I'm sorry I said—
what I said about your family.
You were right.
I was selfish.
And confused.
I think—
I think they're arresting him.
Right now.
By Wyland.
I'm sorry."

She doesn't say a word.

DEFLATE

I wait a second longer,
hope leaking out of me
like air.
I start walking
to my own car.

RIGHT

"Did you tell Dougie
to try not to screw it up?"
She ruffles her pink hair.
Throws her bag in the trunk.

I smile.
"He seemed to know
what he was doing."

She rolls her eyes.
"Do you have work tonight?"

I shake my head.

"Alright, so what
are we doing?
Water tower?
My basement?
Road trip to Vegas?"

Not everything feels right
in my world,
but at least
this does.

NOT YET

"I was thinking
we could text Lindsay," I say.
"See what she's up to."

Lex pulls out her phone and lexts.
Suddenly, she catches me
in a side-hug.

"I missed you, Maypole.
Do you want to
talk about
any of it?"

I know she's talking
about what's happening to my dad
on the other side of town
as we speak.

"Nope.
Not yet."

"Okay."

We wait for Lindsay
to text back.

FIVE MONTHS LATER

HIS DAUGHTER

My hands grip
the edges
of the podium.
I stare out at the sea
of black caps and gowns,
of sweating parents and grandparents.

I can almost hear the whispers:
You know who that is,
don't you?

Ed Morris's girl.

Yes, the killer they picked up
right here in town.

DNA was a perfect match.

No, the trial doesn't start
for months.

That's his daughter.

VALEDICTORIAN'S ADDRESS TO THE SENIOR CLASS

"There was a time this year
when I stopped believing
that this would happen
for me.
That I could
or should
be standing here
before you today.
That I would graduate
at all."

A hush falls.
I grip
the podium
tighter.

LIFTING

"But I was fortunate enough
to have others
who lifted me up
when I could barely
drag myself through the day."

Light winks off of
Lindsay's glasses
in the back.
I spot Davey
a few rows closer.
He smiles encouragingly at me
even now.
Then Doc Anderson,
who sits with folded hands
and a small smile.

"They reminded me
that I am in charge
of who I am.
I get to shape
my own narrative."
My eyes cut to Raquel Tanner.
She stares at her feet.

"And so do you.
We may borrow
from the people who've raised us
or left us,
the experiences that have molded
or scarred us.
But that isn't where it ends.

186

Where *we* end."

I squint toward the bleachers.
I know my mom is up there,
tears in her eyes
that she will not wipe away.

PROOF

"Take my standing here today
as proof
that we get to decide
who we want to become.
Take a moment
to savor
the power in that,
the freedom."

Pictures of college dorms
and studying abroad
and giant labs
dance before me.

"We don't know
what lies ahead for us.
The best we can do
is forge our own paths
and help each other
when we can."

For a moment,
I imagine I see
Brittany Leigh Bates
sitting in the front row.

THE START

"Congratulations,
Jolene High's Class of 2023.
I leave you at the start
of your own story."

Lex's whoop rings out
the second I step back.

The field erupts
in applause.

LAST TRIP TO THE WATER TOWER

That night,
I sit between
Lex and Lindsay.
We swing our legs back and forth
in the empty air.
Jolene lies before us,
nestled in night.

"We're so close,"
says Lindsay.

Just a few more summer weeks
until this whole town
is in our past.

I smile
into the darkness.
Take a deep breath.

I picture the three of us
running from the water tower
through the tall, tall grass.

We don't look back.

WANT TO KEEP READING?

If you liked this book, check out another
book from West 44 Books:

RIGHT ON CUE
BY SABINE BRADLEY

ISBN: 9781978596160

MOVIES ARE MOSTLY PREDICTABLE

That's what I like about them.

    A lost hero is sure to be found.
    Uncertain hearts will, over time,
let each other in.

    The storms are easy to predict.
    I can tell how things will end.
No twist I can't see coming.

I like it that way.

I'VE NEVER BEEN TO NEW YORK

I hear you could live there

     your whole life and

never see the same face twice.

I hear the city stays up

     yelling your name

from the sidewalk.

I hear every brick wall

     and park bench

is a canvas.

WORTH

I hear that's the place to go

    if you want to be

anyone worth

    remembering.

Through art.

Through some mural.

Or even film.

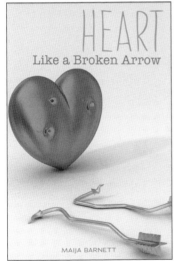

CHECK OUT MORE BOOKS AT:
www.west44books.com

An imprint of Enslow Publishing

WEST **44** BOOKS™

About the Author

Paige Classey is a school librarian who lives
with her husband and son on the Connecticut
shoreline. Her articles on libraries and education
have appeared in School Library Journal,
TEACH Magazine, and Education Week.
This is her first novel.